Elana's Ears

or How I Became
the Best Big Sister
in the World

Published by
MAGINATION PRESS
An Educational Publishing Foundation Book
American Psychological Association
750 First Street, NE
Washington, DC 20002

For more information about our books, including a complete catalog,
please write to us, call 1-800-374-2721, or visit our website at www.maginationpress.com

The text type is Stone Informal
Printed by Phoenix Color, Rockaway, New Jersey
Editor: Darcie Conner Johnston
Art Director: Susan K. White

Library of Congress Cataloging-in-Publication Data

Lowell, Gloria Roth.
Elana's ears, or How I became the best big sister in the world / by Gloria Roth Lowell ;
illustrated by Karen Stormer Brooks.
    p.   cm.
Summary: Lacey the family dog is jealous of the new baby that her human parents
brought home, until she discovers that the baby cannot hear.
ISBN 1-55798-598-7 (hardcover).—ISBN 1-55798-702-5 (paperback).
[1. Dogs—Fiction. 2. Hearing impaired—Fiction. 3. Physically handicapped—Fiction.]
I. Title: How I became the best big sister in the world.
II. Brooks, Karen Stormer, ill. III. Title.
PZ7.L96454 E1 2000   99-045320
[E]—dc21   CIP

Manufactured in the United States of America
10 9 8 7 6 5 4 3 2 1

Elana's Ears

or How I Became
the Best Big Sister
in the World

WRITTEN BY
Gloria Roth Lowell

ILLUSTRATED BY
Karen Stormer Brooks

BARK!

MAGINATION PRESS · WASHINGTON, DC

A Note About Elana's Ears

Hearing loss is one of the most frequent conditions to occur in newborns, and almost 15 percent of all school-age children have some degree of hearing impairment. Like Elana, the average age at which children in the United States are diagnosed with hearing loss is around two years. Studies show, however, that earlier detection and treatment greatly enhance a child's ability to acquire language and social skills, and that children who receive appropriate treatment before the age of six months can develop these crucial life skills as well as their hearing peers. Many health organizations, including the American Academy of Pediatrics and the National Institutes of Health, therefore recommend that all children be screened for hearing loss at birth.

For you, Elana,
with love and admiration — GRL

For Connor and Holly,
who love their pets too — KSB

The story I am about to tell you is true. My name is Lacey, and as you can see from my floppy ears and fuzzy face, I'm a dog. I really don't do many tricks, and I've never saved a life like one of those superdogs you see on TV. But one thing I can do really well is bark. I practice a lot to keep my skill up, and besides, I just love it. I truly believe it's the perfect hobby for any dog, large or small.

I had a wonderful life as an only pet for four fantastic years. I mean, I was living large. I had my own room and my own doggie raincoat that I kept in my own closet. Whenever my parents went on vacation, they took me along. Did you know that some hotels don't allow dogs? What nerve.

Well, a while back I noticed that my mom's belly was getting pretty large. "Hey, lay off the pizza and Chinese food," I thought to myself, but I didn't whimper a word. You know how sensitive moms and dads can be about that sort of thing. Then, a couple of weeks later my parents went away, and they didn't take me. They just rushed out in the middle of the night without even saying goodbye. Where were they? Hey, what was going on here? This was no way to treat a dog.

When they finally came home, they were carrying
something that was making a lot of noise. It was
wrapped in so much pink fluff my eyes hurt just looking
at it. And then I realized what was under that pink
fluff. Can you guess? Yes, they had gone and had a
baby on me! How did I miss it? The other dogs in the
neighborhood had warned me about this day. I had a
deep feeling that my life was about to change big time.

My feeling couldn't have been more right.   My life did change.
My room, the room I lived in for four years by myself, had to be shared.
I had only one little corner to myself.   The kid got everything.
Toys, clothes, stuffed animals, and what's more, every time she cried,
Mom or Dad brought her a drink.   This I could not believe.   For four
long years, whenever I wanted a drink, I had to get up and take the
long hike to the kitchen.   Talk about service with a capital "S."

Oh, by the way, the kid's name is Elana. She didn't do much at first, but once she started to grow, she did more things and—okay, I'll admit it—she got to be sort of interesting. Personally speaking, the best thing she did was throw food on the floor. I always helped out Mom and Dad by eating it. It was a tough job, but *somedog's* got to do it.

As I told you, my favorite hobby is barking, and that got me thinking. Maybe the kid could learn something if I showed her. So when I was around Elana, I started to bark a lot. I was hoping that she would share my hobby so the two of us could howl our brains out. But you know what? Elana never looked at me when I barked. I would stand behind her and bark my head off, but she wouldn't even turn around. This was making me crazy.

One thing about us dogs is that we have really
great hearing. I can hear Dad coming up the
sidewalk from way down the street, and I used
to bark at Elana to come to the door and greet
him with me. Maybe we could even race,
I was thinking. But she never followed.

12

One day when Mom was cooking and I was playing block towers with Elana in the kitchen, Mom dropped a big pot. Oh, what a noise! But Elana didn't even notice. I mean, my ears are still ringing to this day, but there she was, just going about her business stacking one block on top of another. That's when I began to think that maybe Elana's ears weren't working the way they're supposed to.

I had to try and tell my parents. For weeks, I barked
and barked and barked around Elana to show Mom and
Dad that she wasn't looking. I barked so much my throat
got sore. Finally (moms and dads can be kind of slow
sometimes) I heard them talking about Elana's ears, and
the very next day they took her to the doctor. That was
the second time in my life they didn't say goodbye.

When they came home, both of my parents were upset. You know how you can always tell when your parents are upset. I heard them call Grandma Renee and Grandpa Al to tell them the news I already knew in my heart. Elana's ears weren't working. Elana couldn't hear.

I'm going to tell you something now that I've never told anyone else in the world, and I'm going to trust you to keep it to yourself. Do you promise? Okay, here goes. I had been a little jealous of Elana since she came to live in my room. Okay, okay, I was *extremely* jealous!

She got almost all of the attention. This girl had it made—parents who loved her, toys, all the food and drink she wanted. Since the day she came into my room, I'd been second fiddle. Sure, they'd walk me and play with me, but honestly, it wasn't the same. I was jealous. When you're jealous, it means that you want something that someone else has. But then I started to think. If Elana knew about hearing, would she be jealous of me because I could hear really well and she couldn't? I hoped not. I mean, I wished I could give her some of my hearing.

That night as I lay down in my bed next to Elana's, I thought some more. Mom and Dad said they were going to get Elana the help she needed. I started to think about how I could help, too. I'm six years old (that's forty-two in dog years). That makes me pretty wise, right? I should be able to figure something out. I could barely sleep, which for a dog is highly unusual.

When I woke up, I remembered a dream I had. We were in our
own neighborhood, and I was standing on a corner talking to
a friend about a new fire hydrant that had just been installed.
There was a big truck coming around the corner. And just then,
Elana decided to cross the street all by herself.

When I saw what was happening, I realized Elana couldn't hear
the truck honking its horn at her. I dashed down the sidewalk
and reached her just in time to flop my long ears over hers.
In my dream, she heard the truck and ran to the other side of
the street without a moment to spare.

After that dream a great idea came to me. I knew
how I could help. I would be Elana's ears. I'd follow
her everywhere. Sometimes people who can't see
have seeing-eye dogs. Well, I would be Lacey, the
First Ever Hearing-Ear Dog. It would be an even
tougher job than cleaning ice cream and spaghetti
off the floor, but I was up for it.

Wherever Elana went, I went. If there was a knock at the door, I ran to the door. If she was playing with something that she shouldn't, I ran to Mom and Dad and barked so they'd realize Elana was in danger. I followed her everywhere, and let me tell you, I was wearing myself out. The kid never wanted to lounge around in a nice cozy chair or in front of a sunny window. No, she'd rather push her shopping cart around and around the house until my head was spinning.

One day Elana came home with something
bigger than Mom's earrings hooked
around her ears. She was
watching Mom put away her
coat when I practiced a few barks
behind her, just to keep up with
my hobby. But this time when
I barked, Elana turned around
and smiled. I couldn't believe it!
I barked again, and the kid
smiled again! "Yes, Lacey,"
Mom laughed, and scratched
my favorite place on my neck,
"Elana can hear her big sister now."
Big Sister, I thought to myself,
now there's a title I can work with.

22

Turns out Elana got something called hearing aids to wear around her ears and help her hear. You should have seen my little sister Elana. A whole new world opened up to her. With her hearing aids she could hear music and voices on TV and horns honking, and she could hear Mom, Dad, and Yours Truly, Lacey, the Big Sister and First Ever Hearing-Ear Dog for the first time. She wasn't able to understand us at first, but after awhile she could, and pretty soon she started to say words, too. She goes to a special teacher who helps her learn to talk. "No" is a real big word for her now. She likes saying it almost as much as I like to bark.

When Elana visits her teacher, I wait by the door for her to come home and play. She loves to dance and I love to sing (it's closely related to my favorite hobby), so we have Mom put on some music and we dance and sing until she gets dizzy. Then we roll around on the rug and play tug-of-war with my doggie rope. Sometimes she tickles me, which I really like, even though I pretend to growl at her. Elana's favorite thing to do, however, is to tell me to stop barking. Imagine that!

Being Elana's ears has gotten easier since she got her hearing aids. I still pay extra attention when she takes a bath or goes swimming, though, because she doesn't wear her hearing aids in the water and can't hear. So there I am, standing guard, all ears, on my toes, ready for action, and what does she do? You got it. She splashes me right in the face, every time! I don't always like to admit it, but we have a lot of fun together. Things were maybe a little too quiet before she came into my life.

Even sharing a room hasn't turned out to be as terrible as I first thought. Sometimes at night, after Mom and Dad tuck us in, we play tug-of-war under the covers with her socks. Then we get quiet and Elana tells me all about her adventures at the park or her secret hiding place behind the couch or her new dancing shoes.

26

Elana helps me out, too.
She sneaks my water bowl
into our bedroom so I don't
have to walk so far when
I'm thirsty. What a kid!

27

Sometimes when I think about how jealous I was of my little sister I smile and realize how much I love her.   She's even taking up my favorite hobby.   We drive Mom and Dad crazy together.   Don't tell anyone this, but it's more fun to share my hobby with my sister than it was to do it by myself.

So that's my story. I may never be a superdog with my own TV show, but I am Elana's Ears, the First Ever Hearing-Ear Dog and, if I may say so myself, the Best Big Sister in the World.

A Note to Parents About Babies and Older Children

by Jane Annunziata, Psy.D.

What to Expect

A new baby in the family is a source of joy for everyone. Older brothers and sisters usually welcome the arrival with their own brand of excitement, wonder, pride, caring, and affection, just as their parents do. At the same time, however, their world is changing in ways they don't understand and can't control, and along with such changes comes an array of less positive feelings, including:

- anger that they have to share Mom and Dad with someone else and that they are no longer the primary focus of their parents' attention;
- jealousy toward this cute little person who is getting so much attention and admiration from so many people;
- resentment that the parents may not have the same amount of time and energy to devote to them;
- fears that Mom and Dad don't love them as much, now that there is a new baby to "take their place" and love;
- confusion from of all of these competing and conflicting feelings.

When a new baby comes into the household, older children may express their negative feelings in a range of ways, including:

- regression, or behaving like a baby and wanting to be treated like one;
- acting out, such as throwing tantrums, pinching the baby, or breaking the baby's toys or Mom's and Dad's things;
- trying to be the perfect child or the perfect big sister or brother.

These feelings and reactions can be intense—and they are entirely normal, if not inevitable.

What to Do

BEFORE THE BABY ARRIVES

- Prepare your older child or children before the new baby arrives, and start earlier rather than later. Even very young children are aware that something is afoot when parents start talking more in private, or when Mom is always tired or her lap is disappearing. Advance work goes a long way toward easing children's adjustment to the baby and lays a strong foundation for absorbing the many feelings and behaviors that are inevitable with the new arrival.

- Plan for the birth itself. Visit the hospital before the birth so that your child has a visual image of where you are going to be. Many hospitals offer classes and tours for siblings, which can further de-mystify the event for them and decrease their anxiety. Let your children know who will be caring for them, how long Mom will be gone, when Dad will be home, when they can visit Mom in the hospital, and so on. Concrete, visual reminders are especially reassuring; for example, write out the plan for your child and post it prominently. Even children who are too young to read are reassured by its very existence and can ask to have it read (and reread) to them.

AFTER THE BABY ARRIVES

- Set aside as much one-on-one time with each older child as possible. Even if it's just 15 minutes a day or one afternoon a week, it is important that he or she has some exclusive time with Mom and Dad, separately and together, without having to share that time with the baby. Tell your older child how glad you are to have this special time just with him or her.

- Remind your older children often of their special place in the family. Tell them that no one can take their place and that each is a unique person. Also state clearly that the baby is an *addition* to the family and that no one is going away because a new member is arriving.

- Let your older child know that while you love the baby, you also love older children and don't wish that the older child was a baby again or still a baby. Some of the regression that often occurs when a sibling is born is related to the fantasy that goes something like this: "Mom and Dad are so happy with that baby. They must really like babies. Maybe if I act like a baby they'll love me more."

- Tell your children stories about themselves as a baby, and show them photographs, their baby book, and any other mementos you have of their infancy. This will help them feel that they were (and still are) cherished, too, just like the baby.

- Gently and at appropriate moments remind your older child of the many benefits of being "bigger." For example, you can say, "Babies can only drink milk. They don't get to eat ice cream like you do," or "Your sister is too little to go swimming with us; she won't be able to go until she is bigger like you." This will help when your child is feeling jealous or wishes to be a baby.

- Tell your older child that you are thinking of him or her even when you are caring for the baby. This seems so obvious to adults that parents usually don't think to tell their child, but doing so helps ease some of the jealousy that children feel.

- Include your older child in some decisions about the baby, both before and after the arrival. When children have some say in the preparations (for example, "Should we buy a yellow blanket or a striped one?"), they feel more involved. Also, this helps with feelings of lack of control that so often come with the news of a baby, feelings that are typically expressed as, "No one asked me if I wanted a new brother!" Be careful not to overdo, though; this can lead to resentment over all the special purchases and time being spent on the baby.

- In general, the baby should not change things more than necessary. Maintain the same schedules, rituals, and rules you had with your older child, so that the world stays as predictable and stable as possible. Expect to have the rules challenged more than usual.

- In particular, try not to make changes to an older child's bedroom, which can easily result in greater feelings of displacement. If your child's room must be moved, do it several months before the baby arrives, and give him or her as much control as possible in the furnishing and decorating of the new space. If the older child will be sharing a room with the baby, again involve him or her in the process to the greatest extent possible. Try to keep older children from feeling shunted to a corner of the room, and help them maintain a sense that it is still their room. Even a simple line of masking tape on the floor or a curtain hanging in the middle of the room preserves a sense that "at least part of this is still mine."

Explain to your older children what a baby can and cannot do, so that they know what to expect and their fantasies aren't disappointed. An ideal way to do this is to cuddle up with them and read together from the many available books and pamphlets that list babies' development month by month. This will also give you an opportunity to reminisce with each child about what he or she was like as a baby or toddler.

Ask your child for help from time to time. He or she can bring you a diaper, sing a song to the baby, help sort laundry, and so on. If children ask to push the stroller or hold the baby, facilitate their being able to do so safely, making sure rules are clear. Such involvement fosters the older child's feelings of importance and belonging, and helps establish sibling bonds.

Avoid giving your child too much responsibility, which can cause resentment. Alternatively, an older child may seek excessive responsibility, imagining that he or she needs to be your perfect little helper to keep or win your love. Reassure such children that you love them just the way they are, and that having the new baby will never change that. Also, it may be a relief to them if you state directly that being the parent is your job, and theirs is still being a child, even if they are big brothers and sisters now. Like Lacey in this story, they can feel proud of being a good big sister or brother, but they should not feel anxious that they need to perform to perfection.

Offer alternatives when your children can't do something they want to do or used to be able to do because of the baby. For example, when the baby is sleeping and the older child must be quiet, devise activities that are suitable and fun, such as baking something, painting or drawing, or reading a book together.

Listen to your older children. It is not uncommon for them, especially younger ones, to make strong statements such as, "I wish that baby had never been born! I hate him!" or "I want to throw that baby in the trashcan." Of course, older children should not be permitted to harm the baby, but it is important that they be allowed to express their feelings verbally. As a parent, you can absorb these statements and use them as opportunities to define limits with the child and help him or her find constructive ways to deal with anger. For example, you might say, "Well, you certainly can't throw the baby in the trash or hurt her in any way, but I'm glad you can tell me how angry you feel toward her. Let's think of some better ways to get out the angry feelings. Maybe you can draw a picture of them, or punch a pillow. Also, let's figure out what's making you feel so annoyed right now. I bet that will help, too."

Address as much as possible your child's valid complaints about the baby. For example, if the baby's crying wakes your older child at night, look for solutions with the child, such as shutting the bedroom door after he or she is asleep or running a noise-screen such as a fan in the room. By responding in this way, children not only hear that there is a potential solution to the problem, but even more important, they can see that their parents are devoted to meeting *their* needs and not just the baby's.

When the going gets rough, as it often does, it may help to remember that your child is behaving in ways that are to be expected. In the same way, it can even be calming to the child to be told directly, "It's okay to feel mad at your new brother sometimes. All children feel that way when they are getting used to a new brother or sister."

Jane Annunziata, Psy.D., is a clinical psychologist with a private practice for children and families in McLean, Virginia. She is also an author of several books that address the special concerns of children and parents.